New
Hampshire
Maine
Vermont
Minnesota
Wisconsin
Michigan
New York
Massachusetts
Rhode Island
Connecticut
Iowa
Pennsylvania
New Jersey
Ohio
Delaware
Illinois
Indiana
West
Virginia
Maryland
Washington, D.C.
Virginia
Missouri
Kentucky
North Carolina
Tennessee
ahoma
Arkansas
South Carolina
Mississippi
Alabama
Georgia
Louisiana
Florida
N
W
E
S

MINNESOTA
Isle Royale
Lake Superior
ONTARIO,
CANADA
Marquette
Escanaba
River
Mackinac
Island
Mackinac
Bridge
Iron Mountain
Lake Huron
WISCONSIN
Sturgeon
Point
Lighthouse
Sleeping Bear
Dunes National
Lakeshore
Lake Michigan
Muskegon River
N
W
E
S
Grand Rapids
Lansing
Holland
Grand River
Detroit River
Detroit
Ann Arbor
Lake Erie
ILLINOIS
OHIO
INDIANA

The Twelve Days of Christmas in Michigan

written by
Susan Collins Thoms

illustrated by
Deb Pilutti

STERLING
New York / London

Dear Katie,

Hold out your right hand with your palm facing you. Believe it or not, you are looking at a map of Michigan's Lower Peninsula. Can you see why this is called the Mitten State? In the middle of your palm is Lansing—the state's capital and my hometown.

Now, hold your left hand sideways, above your right hand. That looks a bit like Michigan's Upper Peninsula.

The map you hold in your hands is our gift to you. We are bringing you to Michigan for the twelve days of Christmas!

We are going to see as much of this state as we can. Trust me, there's a lot to see. This is the Great Lakes State and a winter wonderland! We have Motor City and Furniture City, sand dunes and ski hills, Yoopers and Trolls (that might not make sense now, but it will soon).

So, pack your bags, grab some snow boots, and rev your engines. You're in for a wild trip.

Your favorite cousin,

Will

Dear Mom and Dad,

Hello from Michigan! I see why they call this state a winter wonderland. When I arrived at the airport in Lansing last night, fat, fluffy snowflakes were falling and a thick blanket of snow covered the ground. Even though the air was shivery cold, everything looked cozy.

This morning, Will said he wanted to go for a hike behind his house. I thought it would be impossible to wade through the deep snow, but I was wrong. We wore snowshoes, which let us float on top of the snow!

Uncle Mike says that snowshoes were invented by the Native Americans. The ancestors of Michigan's Indians came here 14,000 years ago. A lot of Native Americans still live in Michigan, including the People of the Three Fires—the Ottawa, the Ojibwa, and the Potawatomi.

On our hike, we saw an enormous white pine, Michigan's state tree. Will said you can tell it's a white pine because the needles are long and soft and grow in groups of five. We also saw a robin, the state bird. Will was really surprised because most robins head south in the winter. Maybe this robin thinks the snow is pretty, too!

Love,

Katie

P.S. Um . . . is there room in our front yard for one more tree? When you see the presents Will gave me, you'll understand why I'm asking.

On the first day of Christmas,
my cousin gave to me . . .

a robin in a white pine tree.

Beep! Beep!

We visited Detroit today. It's called Motor City. Everywhere I looked, there were shiny cars zipping down streets, roaring down expressways. Aunt Barb said Detroit is home to the Big Three American auto companies—General Motors, Ford, and Chrysler.

We drove down a famous road called Woodward Avenue. Uncle Mike said that in 1909, Woodward had the first mile of rural concrete highway in the country.

Next, we went to the Henry Ford Museum. It has more cars than I could count! I learned about the assembly line, which Henry Ford perfected to build the Model T quickly and keep the cost low. He could build a whole car in 93 minutes and sell it for only $300.

We took a ride in a Model T around Greenfield Village, an old-fashioned village that was decorated for Christmas. I begged the guide to let me get behind the wheel, but he said driving was his job. How old do I have to be to get a driver's license?

Love,

Katie

On the second day of Christmas,
my cousin gave to me . . .

2 Model Ts

and a robin in a white pine tree.

Hi, Mom and Dad.

Will is nuts about lighthouses, and he loves ghost stories. I guess he lives in the right state. There are more than 115 lighthouses in Michigan, and there are lots of spooky stories to go with them.

Today we drove north to Lake Huron to visit the Sturgeon Point Lighthouse. It was built in 1869 to warn ships away from a dangerous reef. A keeper lived in the cabin and kept the light burning all night, every night.

Now the light runs on electricity, and the keeper's cabin is a museum. I thought it would be fun to live in that pretty white house until Will told me that the lights turn on all by themselves at night. Some people think a keeper's ghost is there, still doing his job.

Sure enough, as we drove away, we saw a light flicker on in the second story window. What a shivery souvenir!

Covered in goose bumps,

Katie

On the third day of Christmas,
my cousin gave to me . . .

3 gray ghosts

2 Model Ts,
and a robin in a white pine tree.

Dear Mom and Dad,

Today I laced up a pair of skates, stepped out on the ice and . . . fell flat on my bottom. You have no idea how hard—and cold—ice is until you land on it!

We skated on a little lake in the middle of "the mitten." Michigan is called the Great Lakes State because it touches four of the five Great Lakes, but it has lots of smaller lakes, too. Aunt Barb says they are a gift of the glaciers. Millions of years ago, big sheets of ice moved across the state, tearing holes in the land. The glaciers melted, filling the holes with water, and the state was left with more than 11,000 lakes!

I inched along the ice until I learned how to step and glide, step and glide. Then Will gave me a hockey stick and a puck and soon I was taking shots at the goal. I even made one!

Hockey is big in Michigan. Will hopes to play hockey for the Detroit Red Wings someday. I asked him what he would do if he didn't make the team. No problem, he said. Maybe he'll play baseball for the Tigers or football for the Lions or basketball for the Pistons.

If you love sports, it sounds like Michigan is the place to be.

Working on my slap shot,

Katie

On the fourth day of Christmas,
my cousin gave to me . . .

4 hockey sticks

3 gray ghosts, 2 Model Ts,
and a robin in a white pine tree.

Dear Mom and Dad,

Did you know Will is a Troll?

Today we drove across the Mighty Mac—the Mackinac Bridge—to get to the Upper Peninsula. It's five miles long, one of the longest suspension bridges in the world.

Michiganders call the Upper Peninsula the U.P., and they call the people who live there Yoopers. Get it? U.P.—Yoopers? The Yoopers sometimes call people from the Lower Peninsula Trolls because they live below the bridge.

High on the Mighty Mac, I could see two of the Great Lakes: Huron and Michigan. They really are great! I felt like I was looking at the ocean but without the salty smell.

Aunt Barb says there are six quadrillion gallons of water in the Great Lakes. They provide drinking water for 40 million people. The biggest, deepest, and coldest is Superior. The smallest two are Erie and Ontario. All the lakes but Ontario touch Michigan.

Those lakes sure looked icy today. In the summer, Will said he swims, fishes, sails, and plays in the Great Lakes. We won't have time to visit all five, but Will figured out a way for me to bring home a little piece of them anyway!

Already planning to come back in July,

Katie

On the fifth day of Christmas, my cousin gave to me . . .

5 frozen lakes

4 hockey sticks, 3 gray ghosts, 2 Model Ts, and a robin in a white pine tree.

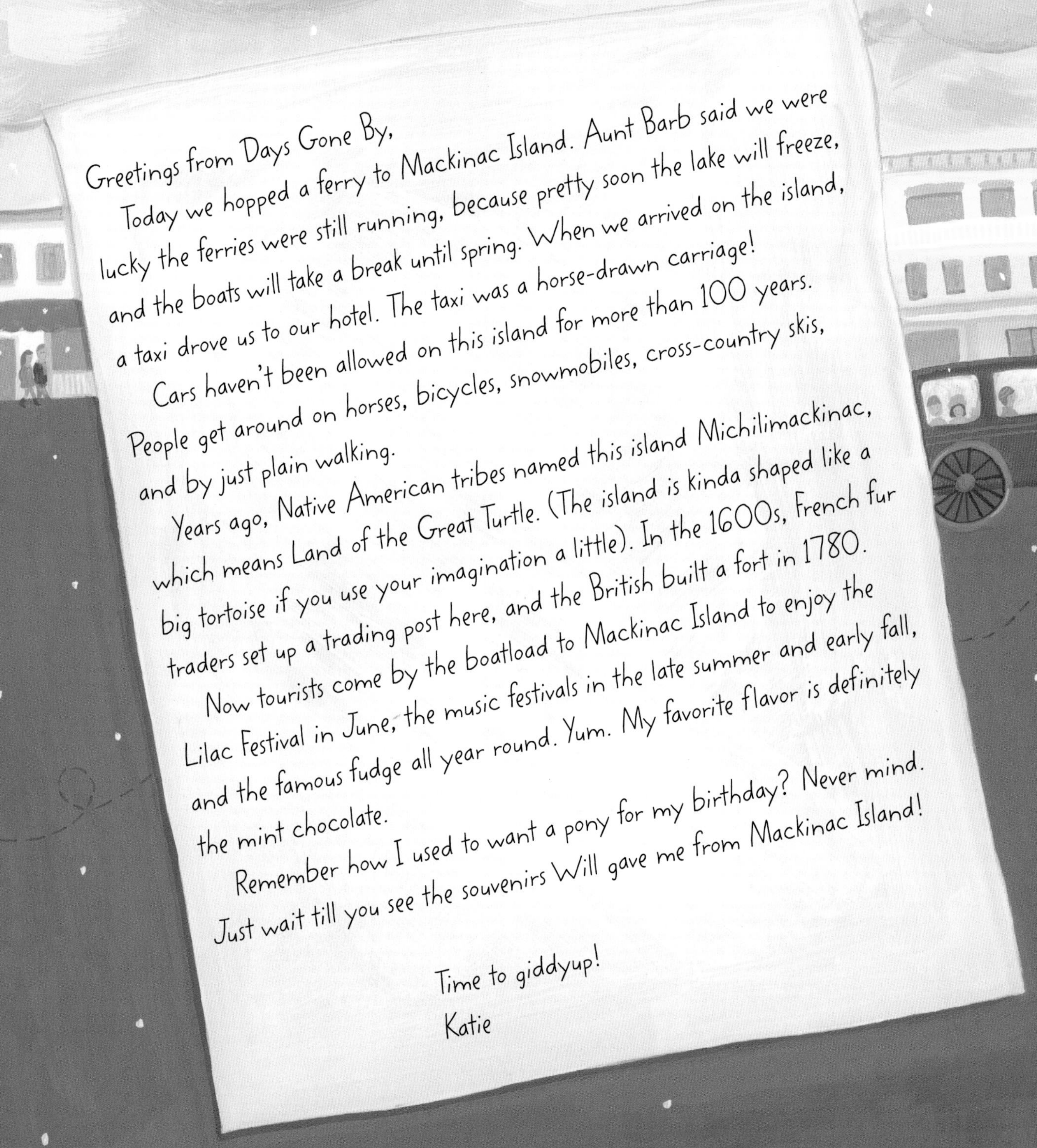

Greetings from Days Gone By,

Today we hopped a ferry to Mackinac Island. Aunt Barb said we were lucky the ferries were still running, because pretty soon the lake will freeze, and the boats will take a break until spring. When we arrived on the island, a taxi drove us to our hotel. The taxi was a horse-drawn carriage!

Cars haven't been allowed on this island for more than 100 years. People get around on horses, bicycles, snowmobiles, cross-country skis, and by just plain walking.

Years ago, Native American tribes named this island Michilimackinac, which means Land of the Great Turtle. (The island is kinda shaped like a big tortoise if you use your imagination a little). In the 1600s, French fur traders set up a trading post here, and the British built a fort in 1780.

Now tourists come by the boatload to Mackinac Island to enjoy the Lilac Festival in June, the music festivals in the late summer and early fall, and the famous fudge all year round. Yum. My favorite flavor is definitely the mint chocolate.

Remember how I used to want a pony for my birthday? Never mind. Just wait till you see the souvenirs Will gave me from Mackinac Island!

Time to giddyup!

Katie

On the sixth day of Christmas,
my cousin gave to me . . .

6 horses clopping

5 frozen lakes,
4 hockey sticks, 3 gray ghosts, 2 Model Ts,
and a robin in a white pine tree.

Hi, Mom and Dad.

When we got to Marquette today, we went straight to the harbor so we could see an enormous freighter being loaded with iron ore. Tons of pellets rattled down chutes from the dock into the ship. It was fun to watch—but REALLY noisy!

Uncle Mike says people have been mining iron in the Upper Peninsula since the 1800s. Copper mining goes back even further. Indians dug up copper as early as 5,000 BC to create tools and decorations.

For dinner, we ate a traditional miner's meal: a meat pie called a pasty (pronounced PASS-tee). At the restaurant, we met some miners who told us stories of the old days. They said if a miner's pasty was cold, he would heat it on a shovel over a candle. I wanted to heat my pasty that way, but the waitress said she didn't have any shovels handy.

Could you learn how to make pasties, Mom? Make a lot, please. I am bringing a few friends home for dinner.

Love,

Katie

On the seventh day of Christmas,
my cousin gave to me . . .

MINE

7 hungry miners

6 horses clopping, 5 frozen lakes,
4 hockey sticks, 3 gray ghosts, 2 Model Ts,
and a robin in a white pine tree.

Dear Mom and Dad,

I played so much in the snow today, I feel a little flake-y. Har har.

This morning, we put on cross-country skis and went gliding through the woods near the town of Iron Mountain. It was quiet and peaceful. I felt like I was floating on top of the snow. But that was too slow for Will, so we went to a ski hill to snowboard. It was faster—but scarier!

Will says that a man from Michigan named Sherman Poppen created one of the earliest snowboards in the 1960s for his daughters. He called it a "snurfer" because it surfed over snow.

We slipped, slid, and shredded down the hills all afternoon. By then, I was ready to just sit down and rest. "Good idea," Will said. He handed me a helmet and told me to sit down—on a snowmobile.

Michigan has more snowmobiles than any other state, so of course I had to go for a ride. Woo hoo! If I lived in the U.P., I would go everywhere by snowmobile.

Your favorite snow bunny,

Katie

On the eighth day of Christmas,
my cousin gave to me . . .

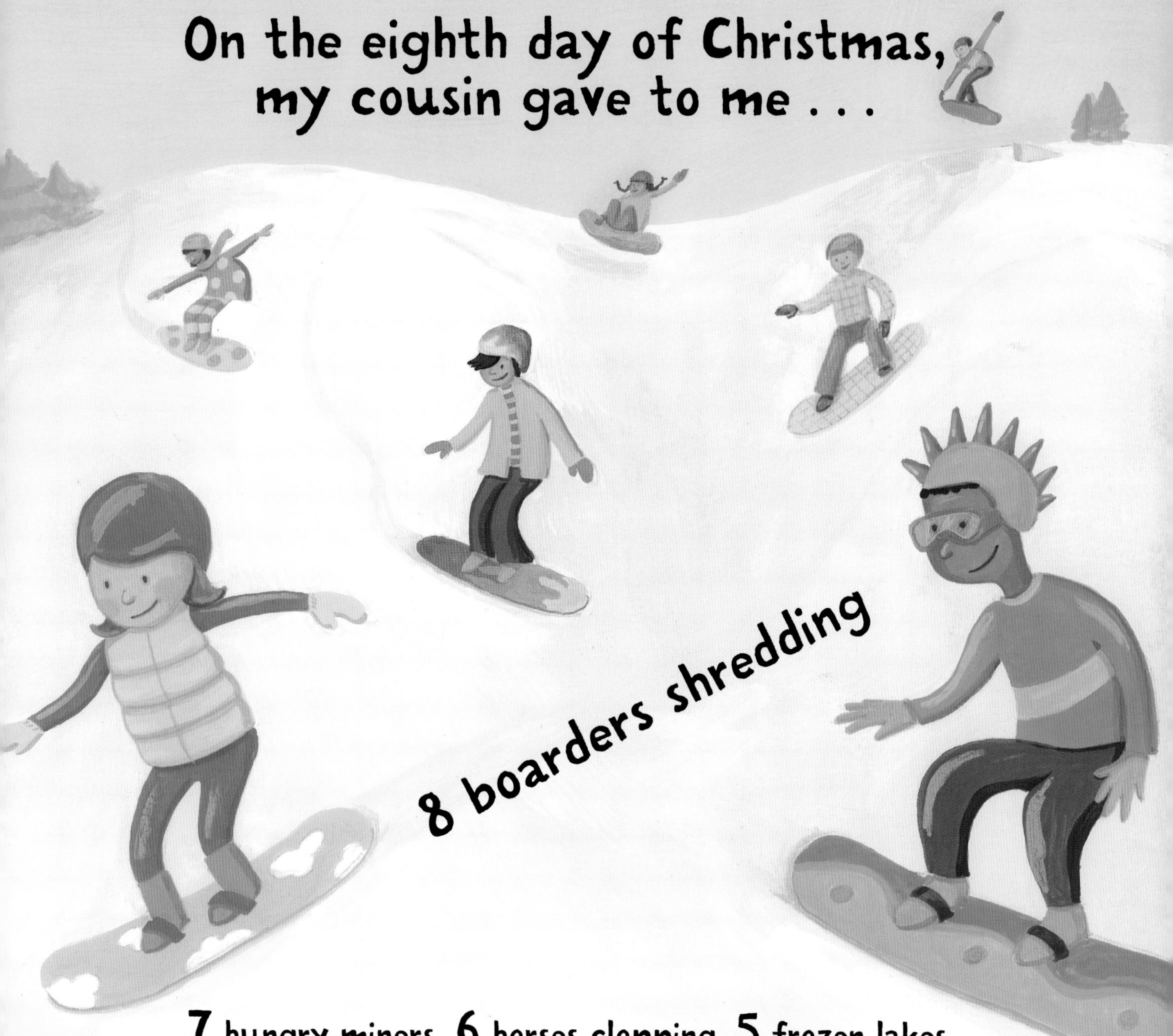

8 boarders shredding

7 hungry miners, 6 horses clopping, 5 frozen lakes,
4 hockey sticks, 3 gray ghosts, 2 Model Ts,
and a robin in a white pine tree.

Dear Mom and Dad,

I think they should call Michigan the Sandbox State. If you saw the huge dunes here, you would know what I mean.

Today, we visited Sleeping Bear Dunes. Its name comes from an Ojibwa Indian legend. A mother bear and two cubs tried to cross Lake Michigan to escape a forest fire. The mother bear reached shore first. She collapsed and waited for her cubs, but they never made it.

The Great Spirit took pity on the poor mother bear. He raised two islands where the cubs had slipped beneath the waves. He covered the mother bear with sand, creating a dune in the shape of a sleeping bear.

It's a sad story, but I must admit I had fun climbing that sandy, snowy dune. I liked running down it even more!

In the afternoon, we hiked along Lake Michigan. I picked up a dusty gray stone with a six-sided pattern on it and almost tossed it in the water. "Are you crazy?" Will said. "That's our state stone!"

Turns out I had found a Petoskey stone. It's a fossil found only in Michigan.

Your #1 cub,

Katie

On the ninth day of Christmas,
my cousin gave to me . . .

9 golden sand dunes

8 boarders shredding, 7 hungry miners, 6 horses clopping,
5 frozen lakes, 4 hockey sticks, 3 gray ghosts, 2 Model Ts,
and a robin in a white pine tree.

Dear Mom and Dad,

Today was a very fruit-ful day. We traveled along the west side of the state and saw acres and acres of fruit farms. Lake Michigan makes the climate here perfect for growing apples, cherries, peaches, pears, plums, blueberries, strawberries, and grapes.

Of course, those crops are not actually growing in the wintertime, but we visited a cider mill and watched apple cider being made. Bushels of apples were fed into a mill and chopped into little pieces. Layers of mushed-up apples were wrapped in cloth and stacked on top of each other. Then, a press slowly pushed down on the apples. Juice poured out by the gallons.

I couldn't wait to try the cider. It tasted cold and crisp, like a fall day. Mmmm. I liked it so much, Will is sending me home with 10 jugs of cider—enough for the whole neighborhood! And he gave me my very own cider press, so I can make more cider whenever I want.

Love,
Katie

On the tenth day of Christmas,
my cousin gave to me . . .

10 jugs of cider

9 golden sand dunes, 8 boarders shredding,
7 hungry miners, 6 horses clopping, 5 frozen lakes,
4 hockey sticks, 3 gray ghosts, 2 Model Ts,
and a robin in a white pine tree.

Hallo, Moeder! Hallo, Vader!

Step, kick. Step, kick. Don't mind me. I am just practicing a new dance.

We went to Holland, a city founded by Dutch immigrants. We watched a man carve wooden shoes by hand. An artist painted pretty pictures of windmills and flowers on them. Will and I each bought a pair. It was tough to clomp around in those hard, stiff shoes.

A girl in the store told us about Tulip Time, a spring festival that brings a half-million visitors to Holland. Tulips bloom everywhere. Kids dress up in Dutch costumes and wooden shoes and march in a parade, and teenagers perform Klompen Dances.

The girl taught us a few dance steps. Ouch. I told her the shoes hurt my feet. She said dancers wear six to eight pairs of socks for cushioning. (Next time I come, I'll remember to pack extra socks.)

After we left Holland, we headed to Grand Rapids. It got the nickname Furniture City in the 1800s when it became famous for making beautiful wooden furniture. It's also famous for being the first city to add fluoride to its drinking water to prevent cavities.

Tonight, I will dream of wooden shoes, fancy chairs, and white teeth.

Your future Klompen Dancer,

Katie

WELKOM

On the eleventh day of Christmas,
my cousin gave to me . . .

11 Dutch girls dancing

10 jugs of cider, 9 golden sand dunes, 8 boarders shredding,
7 hungry miners, 6 horses clopping, 5 frozen lakes,
4 hockey sticks, 3 gray ghosts, 2 Model Ts,
and a robin in a white pine tree.

CHERRY TIME

Hi, Mom and Dad.

Will said we would celebrate my last day in Michigan with a social studies lesson. "You gotta be kidding," I said. "I'm on vacation."

He just smiled and poured me a glass of fizzy soda pop. It was Vernors Ginger Ale. Some people say it was the first soda pop ever created. A pharmacist named James Vernor in Detroit made it in the 1800s. He put ginger, vanilla, and spices in an oak barrel, then left to fight in the Civil War. When he came home four years later, he poured a glass and decided it tasted "deliciously different." I bet he liked the way it tickled his nose, too.

The second part of my lesson was a big, gooey ice cream sundae. Will scooped up a pile of ice cream made with milk from Michigan cows. He loaded it with chunks of Mackinac Island Fudge. And he topped it off with cherry sauce because Michigan grows more tart cherries than any other state. I wish social studies at school could be this tasty.

Best of all, Will gave me the sweetest homework: twelve cherry sundaes. I bet you won't mind helping me finish this assignment.

I had so much fun on this trip, but there's a lot more I want to see and do in Michigan. I think we should all come here in the spring. And again in the summer. And maybe next fall, too.

Your official Michigan tour guide,

Katie

On the twelfth day of Christmas,
my cousin gave to me . . .

12 cherry sundaes

11 Dutch girls dancing, 10 jugs of cider, 9 golden sand dunes,
8 boarders shredding, 7 hungry miners, 6 horses clopping,
5 frozen lakes, 4 hockey sticks, 3 gray ghosts, 2 Model Ts,
and a robin in a white pine tree.

MICHIGAN MISSE
Michigan
SUPERIOR
ERIE
HURON
ONTARIO

OU ALREADY!

Come Back Again Soon!
TAHQUAMENON FALLS
50,000 gallons of water falling per second
AGRICULTUR
#1 in blueberries, tart cherries, pickl
cucumbers, and 3 types of dry
beans: black, cranberry & dry red
E PLURIBUS UNUM
TUEBOR
CIRCUMSPICE
SAIL THROUGH THE SOO LOCKS
Aretha
QUEEN of SOU
SUMMER CAMP
Home of the 300-year-old MONARCH PINE
HARTWICK PINES LOGGING MUSEUM
Peshawbestown
POW WOW
PICTURED ROCKS National Lakeshore
GWEN FROST
STEVIE WONDER
COLON, MI MAGIC CAPITAL of the World
HELEN THOMAS
First Lady of the Press

AIR ZOO MUSEUM
GO BLUE
Hitsville U.S.A.
MOTOWN
SPARTY
SHIPWRECK
MUSEUM
& Whitefish Point Light Station
PURPLE ROSE
THEATRE
JEFF DANIELS
Actor, Musician & Playwright
Rosa Parks
1913-2005
Renaissance Festival
Joe Louis
1914-1981
Heavyweight Boxing CHAMP
"the Brown BOMBER"
FAMOUS MAGICIAN
HARRY BLACKSTONE
1895-1965
Cereal City
BATTLE CREEK
EMINEM
LIJAH
cCoy
INVENTOR
1844-1929
ISLE ROYALE
MICHIGAN CHALLENGE
BALLOONFEST
LABOR DAY BRIDGE WALK
MYSTERY SPOT

Michigan: The Great Lakes State

Capital: Lansing • **State abbreviation:** MI • **Largest city:** Detroit • **State bird:** the American robin • **State flower:** the apple blossom • **State tree:** the white pine • **State stone:** the Petoskey stone • **State fossil:** the mastodon • **State game mammal:** the white-tailed deer • **State wildflower:** the dwarf lake iris • **State gem:** greenstone (chlorastrolite) • **State reptile:** the painted turtle • **State soil:** Kalkaska sand • **State fish:** the brook trout • **State motto:** "If you seek a pleasant peninsula, look about you."

Some Famous Michiganders:

Thomas Alva Edison (1847–1931) grew up in Port Huron and is credited with perfecting the electric light bulb. His many other inventions include the phonograph and motion picture cameras.

Gerald Ford (1913–2006) grew up in Grand Rapids and became the 38th president of the United States. He was born Leslie Lynch King Jr., and his name was changed after his mother married his stepfather.

Aretha Franklin (1942–) grew up in Detroit. She is a singer, songwriter, and pianist known as "The Queen of Soul." Her most famous songs include "Respect" and "Chain of Fools."

Jacques Marquette (1637–1675) was a French missionary and explorer who founded Michigan's first European settlement in Sault Ste. Marie.

Chief Pontiac, or **Obwandiyag,** (1720–1769) was an Ottawa Indian leader who laid siege to Fort Detroit and led Pontiac's Rebellion against the British in the 1760s.

Harriet Quimby (1875–1912) grew up in Arcadia, and in 1911, she became the first American woman to get a pilot's license. The following year, she was the first woman to fly across the English Channel.

Sojourner Truth (1797–1883) lived in Battle Creek. She was a former slave who spoke out against slavery and worked for women's rights. She was born Isabella Baumfree and took the name Sojourner Truth in 1843.

Chris Van Allsburg (1949–), born in Grand Rapids, is a children's author and illustrator. He won Caldecott Medals for *The Polar Express* and *Jumanji*.

For Bill, a Michigander by birth,
a Yooper at heart.
—S.C.T.

For Tom, Kyle, and Jack, my favorite Michiganders.
—D.P.

Library of Congress Cataloging-in-Publication Data
Thoms, Susan Collins.
The twelve days of Christmas in Michigan / written by Susan Collins Thoms ; illustrated by Deb Pilutti. p. cm.
Summary: On each of the twelve days during her Christmas visit with her cousin Will, Katie writes home describing the history, geography, animals, and interesting sites of Michigan that she has explored. Uses the cumulative pattern of the traditional carol to present amusing state trivia at the end of each letter.
ISBN 978-1-4027-6351-9
[1. Michigan–Fiction. 2. Letters–Fiction. 3. Cousins–Fiction. 4. Christmas–Fiction.] I. Pilutti, Deb, ill. II. Title. PZ7.T37372Tw 2010 [Fic] –dc22
2009021852

Lot#:
2 4 6 8 10 9 7 5 3
07/11
Published by Sterling Publishing Co., Inc.
387 Park Avenue South, New York, NY 10016

The original illustrations for this book were painted with gouache.
Distributed in Canada by Sterling Publishing
℅ Canadian Manda Group, 165 Dufferin Street
Toronto, Ontario, Canada M6K 3H6
Distributed in the United Kingdom by GMC Distribution Services
Castle Place, 166 High Street, Lewes, East Sussex, England BN7 1XU
Distributed in Australia by Capricorn Link (Australia) Pty. Ltd.
P.O. Box 704, Windsor, NSW 2756, Australia

Printed in China

Sterling ISBN 978-1-4027-6351-9

For information about custom editions, special sales, premium and corporate purchases,
please contact Sterling Special Sales Department at 800-805-5489 or specialsales@sterlingpublishing.com.

Designed by Kate Moll.

CANADA
Washington
Montana
Oregon
Idaho
Wyoming
Nevada
Utah
Colorado
California
Arizona
New Mexico
Texas
Hawaii
Alaska
MEXICO
(NOT TO SCALE)